This Book Belongs to

_____

The
Dick and Jane
Reading Collection

PENGUIN YOUNG READERS

AN IMPRINT OF PENGUIN RANDOM HOUSE

PENGUIN YOUNG READERS
An Imprint of Penguin Random House LLC

All rights reserved. *Dick and Jane: Go, Go, Go* and *Dick and Jane: Jump and Run* first published in 2003 by Grosset & Dunlap and in 2011 by Penguin Young Readers. *Dick and Jane: We Look* first published in 2003 by Grosset & Dunlap and in 2012 by Penguin Young Readers. *Dick and Jane: We Play* first published in 2004 by Grosset & Dunlap and in 2012 by Penguin Young Readers. This special markets edition published in 2019 by Penguin Young Readers, an imprint of Penguin Random House LLC, 1745 Broadway, New York, New York 10019. Manufactured in Dongguan, China. December 2019.

The Library of Congress has cataloged the individual books under the following Control Numbers:
Dick and Jane: Go, Go, Go: 2003016959, *Dick and Jane: Jump and Run*: 2003016956,
Dick and Jane: We Look: 2003016954, *Dick and Jane: We Play*: 2003016831.

ISBN 9780593089927   10   9   8   7   6   5   4   3

The Dick and Jane
Reading Collection

Dick and Jane
We Look

Penguin Young Readers
An Imprint of Penguin Random House LLC.

Chapters

Chapter 1
Look

Look, look.

Oh, oh, oh.

Oh, oh.

Oh, look.

Chapter 2
Jane

Oh, Jane.

Look, Jane, look.

Look, look.

Oh, look.

See Jane.

See, see.

See Jane.

Oh, see Jane.

Chapter 3
Dick

Look, Jane.

Look, look.

See Dick.

See, see.

Oh, see.

See Dick.

Oh, see Dick.

Oh, oh, oh.

Funny, funny Dick.

Chapter 4
Sally

Look, Dick.

Look, Jane.

See Sally.

Oh, oh, oh.

Oh, Dick.

See Sally.

Look, Jane.

Look, Dick.

See funny Sally.

Funny, funny Sally.

Chapter 5
Big and Little

Come, come.

Come and see.

See Father and Mother.

Father is big.

Mother is little.

Look, Father.

Dick is big.

Sally is little.

Big, big Dick.

Little Baby Sally.

Oh, look, Jane.

Look, Dick, look.

Sally is big.

Tim is little.

Big, big Sally.

Little Baby Tim.

Chapter 6
The Funny Baby

Come down, Dick.

Come and see.

See the big, big mother.

See the funny little baby.

Puff is my baby.

Puff is my funny little baby.

I see the big mother.

I see the little baby.

Look, Jane.

See the big father.

Look, Dick, look.

See something funny.

See my baby jump.

See my baby run.

Oh, oh, oh.

Chapter 7
Something Blue

Oh, Jane, I see something.

I see something blue.

Come and see Mother work.

Mother can make something.

Something blue.

Look, Mother, look.

I can work.

I can make something.

I can make something yellow.

Look, look.

See something yellow.

Oh, Jane, I can work.

I can make something blue.

I can make something yellow.

Oh, see my funny Tim.

Little Tim is yellow.

Baby Sally is blue.

Dick and Jane
We Play

Penguin Young Readers
An Imprint of Penguin Random House LLC.

Chapters

Chapter 1
Play

Oh, Father.

See funny Dick.

Dick can play.

Oh, Mother.

Oh, Father.

Jane can play.

Sally can play.

Oh, Father.

See Spot.

Funny, funny Spot.

Spot can play.

Chapter 2
See Dick Play

Look, Jane.

Look, look.

Look and see.

See Father play.

See Dick play.

Look, Mother.

Look, Mother, look.

See Father.

See Father and Dick.

Oh, Mother.

See Spot.

Look, Mother, look.

Spot can help Dick.

Chapter 3
Funny Spot

Come, Spot.

Come, come.

Play, Spot.

Play, play.

Go, Spot.

Go, go.

Spot can play.

Dick can play.

Oh, oh.

Funny, funny Spot.

Chapter 4
See Spot Play

See Jane jump.

Jump, jump.

See Spot jump.

Jump, jump.

Oh, Dick.

Oh, Jane.

See Spot.

Funny, funny Spot.

Spot can play.

Chapter 5
Funny Father

"Come, Jane," said Father.

"Come and play ball.

Come and play."

"I can help you play ball,"

said Father.

"I can help."

"Come, Father," said Jane.

"Come and play ball.

Come and play."

Oh, funny, funny Father.

Chapter 6
Play Ball

"Come, Jane," said Father.

"Come and play ball.

Come and play."

"Oh," said Jane.

"See the red ball go.

See it go up, up, up.

Run, Dick, run."

"Oh, oh," said Dick.

"Where is my ball?

I can not find it.

Come here, Jane.

Run and help me.

Help me find my red ball."

"I can help you," said Jane.

"We can find the red ball."

Dick said, "I see it.

I see my red ball.

Look, Father.

See where it is.

Come and help me."

Jane said, "Oh, Dick.

Spot can help you.

Spot can find the ball."

Dick and Jane
Go, Go, Go

Penguin Young Readers
An Imprint of Penguin Random House LLC.

Chapters

Chapter 1
Go, Go, Go

Come, Spot.

Come and go.

Jump, jump.

Jump up, Spot.

Jump up.

Oh, Jane.

Look and see.

See Sally go.

See Tim go.

See Spot and Puff go.

75

Oh, Dick.

Look and see.

See Spot jump down.

See Puff jump down.

Down, down, down.

Oh, oh, oh.

Chapter 2
Come

Come, Sally.

Come, come.

Oh, Sally.

Come, come.

Come, Sally, come.

Oh, see.

See Sally go.

Go, Sally, go.

Go, go, go.

Chapter 3
See Jane Go

Oh, Sally.

See Jane go down.

Down, down, down.

See Jane go down.

Look, Jane.

Look, look.

Oh, look.

Look, Tim, look.

Oh, look.

See funny, funny Jane.

See funny Jane go.

Chapter 4
Sally and Mother

Sally said, "Oh, see.

See Mother go.

Come, Dick.

Come, Jane.

Come and go."

Jane said, "Oh, Dick.

See Sally and Tim.

Oh, oh, oh.

See Baby Sally go.

Go, Dick, go."

Sally said, "Oh, Mother.

See Dick go down.

See Jane go down.

Funny, funny Dick and Jane."

Chapter 5
The Boats Go

Oh, Dick.

The blue boat can go.

The yellow boat can go.

My little, red car can go.

Look, look.

See my red car go.

Oh, oh.

See my red car.

See my red car go down.

Down, down, down.

Oh, Dick.

Help, help.

My little, red car is down.

Up, up, up.

Up comes the little, red car.

See Dick help.

See the little, red car come up.

Up, up, up.

The little, red car is up.

Chapter 6
The Big, Red Boat

Come, Baby Sally.

Come and see Father work.

See Father make boats.

The little boat is my boat.

I can make my boat blue.

See my little, blue boat.

Look, Sally, look.

See my big boat.

I can make my boat red.

Look, Sally.

See my boat.

See my big, red boat.

Oh, look, look.

See Puff jump.

See my boat go down.

Oh, look.

My boat is yellow.

Dick and Jane
Jump and Run

Penguin Young Readers
An Imprint of Penguin Random House LLC.

Chapters

Chapter 1
Puff

Jump, Puff.

Jump, jump, jump.

Jump, Puff, jump.

Run, Puff.

Run, Puff, run.

Run, run, run.

Jump, jump, jump.

Oh, Puff.

Oh, oh, oh.

Funny, funny Puff.

Chapter 2
Spot

Come, come.

Come, Spot, come.

Run, run, run.

Jump, Spot.

Jump, jump.

Jump, Spot, jump.

Oh, Spot.

Oh, oh, oh.

Funny, funny Spot.

Chapter 3
Jump and Play

Sally said, "Oh, look.

Mother can jump.

Mother can jump and play."

Dick said, "Jump, Father.

You can jump.

You can jump and play."

"Look, Mother," said Sally.

"See Father jump.

See Father jump and play.

Big, big Father is funny."

Jane said, "Oh, Father.

You can not jump and play.

Spot can not jump and play."

Dick said, "Oh, see Puff.

Puff can jump.

Puff can jump and play."

Chapter 4
Run and Help

Run, Jane.

Help Mother.

Run, Jane, run.

Help Mother work.

Come, Sally, come.

Come and help.

Come and help Mother.

Run, run, run.

Look, Sally, look.

See Spot work.

Funny, funny Spot.

Oh, oh, oh.

Spot can help Mother.

Chapter 5
See Puff Jump

Look, Dick.

See Puff jump.

Oh, look.

Look and see.

See Puff jump and play.

Come, Jane, come.

Come and see Puff.

See Puff jump and run.

See funny, little Puff.

Oh, oh, oh.

See little Puff run.

Oh, see Puff.

Funny, little Puff.

Chapter 6
Spot and Tim and Puff

Spot can jump.

Little Puff can jump.

Look, Tim, look.

See Spot and Puff play.

Look, Tim.

See Sally jump.

See Sally jump down.

Down, down, down.

Sally can jump and play.

Oh, Puff.

See funny, little Tim.

See Tim jump down.

Down, down, down.

Tim can jump and play.

Chapter 7
Oh, See

Look, Sally, look.

Look down.

Look down, Sally.

Look down, down, down.

Look up, Sally.

Look up, up, up.

Run, Sally, run.

Run and jump.

Run and jump up.

Look, Jane.

Look and see.

Oh, see.

See funny, funny Sally.